RATNiP

The Pie-Rat on Seventh Street

BY **CAM HIGGINS** • ILLUSTRATED BY **ALLISON STEINFELD**

LITTLE SIMON
New York Amsterdam/Antwerp London
Toronto Sydney/Melbourne New Delhi

This book is a work of fiction. Any references to historical events, real people, or real places are used fictitiously. Other names, characters, places, and events are products of the author's imagination, and any resemblance to actual events or places or persons, living or dead, is entirely coincidental.

LITTLE SIMON
An imprint of Simon & Schuster Children's Publishing Division
1230 Avenue of the Americas, New York, New York 10020
First Little Simon hardcover edition February 2026
© 2026 by Simon & Schuster, LLC
Also available in a Little Simon paperback edition.
All rights reserved, including the right of reproduction in whole or in part in any form.
LITTLE SIMON is a registered trademark of Simon & Schuster, LLC, and associated colophon is a trademark of Simon & Schuster, LLC.
RATNIP is a trademark of Simon & Schuster, LLC.
For information about special discounts for bulk purchases, please contact Simon & Schuster Special Sales at 1-866-506-1949 or business@simonandschuster.com.
The Simon & Schuster Speakers Bureau can bring authors to your live event. For more information or to book an event, contact the Simon & Schuster Speakers Bureau at 1-866-248-3049 or visit our website at www.simonspeakers.com.
Book design by Brittany Fetcho
Manufactured in the United States of America 1225 LAK
2 4 6 8 10 9 7 5 3 1
CIP data for this book is available from the Library of Congress.
ISBN 9781665988544 (hc)
ISBN 9781665988537 (pbk)
ISBN 9781665988551 (ebook)

Contents

CHAPTER 1: Walking the Plank — 1

CHAPTER 2: Flood City — 15

CHAPTER 3: A Breakfast Bandit — 27

CHAPTER 4: Setting Sail — 37

CHAPTER 5: Treasure Hunting — 51

CHAPTER 6: A New Kind of Pie — 63

CHAPTER 7: Riding the Waves — 75

CHAPTER 8: Shipwrecked — 89

CHAPTER 9: The Seventh Street Swim — 99

CHAPTER 10: Pie, Sweet Pie — 111

CHAPTER 1
WALKING THE PLANK

It was a dark and stormy day.

Really, it was! The sky outside was a grayish green. Thunder crashed, and a howling wind rattled the windows of our pizza parlor home.

RAT FACT: We rats don't mind the rain too much. But this storm was on a whole different level!

The rain poured down in buckets. And speaking of buckets, we were using one to catch the rainwater leaking from the roof.

PLOP PLOP PLOP PLOP PLOP!

When the storm began, Cookie the raccoon told my siblings and me that we needed to stay inside.

We listened, of course. But now we were all getting a little bit bored.

My brother Pepperoni put his paws into the bucket. Then he shook them out near my sister Anchovy and sprayed her with water droplets.

"Hey!" Anchovy squealed.

My other sister, Marg, climbed all the way into the bucket.

First, she floated on her back with her paws folded under her head. Then she stood up and let the rain fall down on her like a shower.

"*Scrub a dub dub,*" she sang as she pretended to scrub her armpits.

We all fell over laughing!

Marg climbed out of the bucket. Now it was my turn to try to make my siblings laugh.

"Watch this!" I said.

I took a running start, somersaulted through the air, and dove headfirst into the bucket.

"Wow!" My siblings hooted and cheered.

"I rate that dive a ten out of ten!" Anchovy called.

But my younger brother, Veggie, shook his head.

"I can do better than that," he said. "Watch! I call this . . . Pirate Walking the Plank!"

Veggie marched along the rim of the bucket with stiff, straight legs. Then, with a yelp, he stepped off the edge and dropped inside the bucket beside me.

Splash!

Veggie cannonballed so hard that he knocked over the entire bucket.

We both tumbled out onto the floor. The water from the bucket sloshed all over the room.

All my brothers and sisters groaned. We knew what this meant.

"Enough playing around," Cookie said as she propped up the bucket again. "Mop up the water, and then off to bed with you all."

"Ratnip and Veggie spilled the water," Pepperoni whined. "So they should clean it up."

I scowled. It wasn't fair. Veggie had spilled the water. Not me!

But Veggie had already gotten down low on his tummy and paws.

"Yar, Ratnip! Let's swab this pirate ship deck clean!" he said.

I sighed. Then I replied, "Aye, aye, Veggie."

So we mopped up the water as fast as we could.

How, you ask? By running around the room and slurping it up like thirsty vacuum cleaners!

But we weren't fast enough to stop the water from seeping into my sock bed.

It takes a lot to gross out a rat. But a wet bed?

Yuck.

CHAPTER 2
FLOOD CITY

When I woke up that night, the storm had quieted down. All I heard was the soft *pat-a-pat-pat* of raindrops tapping lightly on the roof.

I looked around the room. My siblings were yawning and rubbing their eyes as they woke up too. Cookie was nowhere to be seen, though.

"Cookie?" I called out. "Where are you?"

That's when I felt a breeze blowing in through the window.

Strange. That window was always closed. Maybe the wind from the storm had pushed it open?

I was scratching my head when suddenly there was a great big *whoosh*.

Cookie came bursting through the open window. She sailed over our heads and into the room like a Super Raccoon!

What was going on?!

Cookie landed gracefully on all four paws. Her fur glistened with raindrops. Scraps of food tumbled out of her arms.

"It's time for breakfast," she announced. "I brought enough food for everyone."

Why had Cookie burst in through the window? Why weren't we going outside to search for our own breakfasts, like we usually did?

I had so many questions!

Cookie pointed up at the window.

"Go look outside," she said.

My siblings and I climbed onto one another's shoulders until we formed a tall rat chain. I stood perched at the very top, just high enough to peer through the window.

The view I saw from there took my breath away.

"The City has turned into a water wonderland!" I shouted.

Gone were the sidewalks and the streets. Everything had turned into one big puddle. I had never seen anything like it before!

Cookie led us over to the big crack in the wall. We usually used it to go in and out of our house. But now the crack was stuffed full of crumpled fabric and newspapers.

"I filled in the crack so the water wouldn't come inside," Cookie explained. "Until the water goes away, that window is our only way in and out. That's why it was easier for me to get breakfast for everyone tonight."

"Thank you, Cookie!" my siblings and I chimed.

All my whiskers twitched with excitement. Who knew what kind of treasures were waiting outside in The City after the storm?

I couldn't wait to find out!

CHAPTER 3
A BREAKFAST BANDIT

RAT FACT: Exploring is best done on a full stomach. So before I set off on my adventure, I sat down with my family to eat breakfast.

There were corncobs, watermelon rinds, and sandwich crusts. To wash it all down, we had a pickle jar with salty pickle juice inside.

The real star of breakfast was the beans called edamame. Their pods were salty on the outside. If you bit in just the right spot, a slippery green pea would shoot out. Yum!

I wanted to save the best for last, so I first chewed through a corncob. Then I took a good, long sip of the pickle juice. *Mmm.*

Just as I reached to grab the last edamame pod, another paw reached out and snatched it away.

"This edamame is mine!" Veggie squeaked. He sunk his teeth into the pod.

"Hey!" I cried. "That was mine! I haven't eaten ANY edamame yet!"

Veggie finished swallowing.

"Oopsies! That was my third," he said. Then he stuck out his tongue. "Well, you snooze, you lose!"

You know what's worse than no edamame? The promise of edamame . . . and then having it taken away from you!

I huffed my way through the rest of breakfast.

There was only one thing that could make me feel better: treasure hunting on the high seas!

Rats are pretty good swimmers, but I needed something professional for my special exploration.

I hurried up to my treasure room and rummaged around.

"I bet this will work," I said, pulling out a red-and-white checkered paper carton.

The carton was big enough to stand in. It had a special waxy coating that would keep it from falling apart in the water.

Next I picked out a blue-and-white striped straw. I glued it to the middle of the boat with a wad of A-B-C gum. (That stands for "already been chewed.")

Then I tied a napkin from Nonna Pizzeria onto the straw. Now I had my sail!

The ship's rudder was made from a wooden toothpick. A trusty bottle cap became the ship's wheel.

I slid an eye patch onto my head for the finishing touch.

"Ta-da!" I shouted. "Transformation complete!"

I wasn't just any old pirate. I was a *PIE-RAT!*

CHAPTER 4
SETTING SAIL

Cookie helped me hoist my boat up through the window.

Once we were outside, I turned to her and asked, "Permission to set sail for adventure?"

"Set sail, my Ratnip!" Cookie said. "Just stay away from the gutters. The water moves much faster near them."

"Stay away from the gutters," I repeated. "Okay!"

I jumped into my boat and was about to sail off when Veggie appeared.

"Permission to join your crew, Captain?" he said.

Now, any other time, I would have said yes right away.

But I was still annoyed about mopping up the floor and sleeping in my wet bed yesterday. Not to mention that Veggie swiped my edamame at breakfast!

Rat Fact: If we rats hold grudges about anything, it's food.

So I crossed my arms and shook my head.

"Nuh-uh. Pie-rats aren't just playing around," I said. "This is a serious treasure-hunting mission."

"But I'm on a mission too. I'm . . . uh . . ." Veggie's voice trailed off. Then his eyes landed on my pizza napkin sail. "Oh! I'm looking for pizza!"

I sighed. I could tell he was just blurting out the first thing that came to mind.

But I didn't want to waste any more time.

"FINE. You can join," I said. "But my treasure hunting comes first, okay? I'm not going to change the route or wait up for you."

"Yippee!" Veggie cheered and jumped aboard. "I'll be your first mate! Yo ho ho!"

And so Veggie and I sailed off into The City.

By now the rain had stopped completely. A gentle breeze pushed our boat along the streets . . . which were more like streams.

It was funny how just a little bit of water transformed a place. Most of the lights were out too. It felt like Veggie and I had the whole City to ourselves!

"Why is it so quiet, Captain Ratnip?" Veggie asked.

I had the exact same question. I looked around and noticed two things.

First, there were no humans outside.

To be fair, most of them sleep at night while we rats are awake. But tonight, there wasn't a single human in sight.

And second, all the cars were sleeping.

Even at night, there were always a few cars running around the streets with their bright eyes. But now they stood completely still with their tires underwater.

Who knows? Maybe cars don't like swimming.

I sniffed the air and said, "Hey, you know what it smells like out here?"

Veggie clapped his paws with excitement.

"Do you smell pizza?" he said.

"No, Veggie!" I said. "It smells like ADVENTURE!"

CHAPTER 5
TREASURE HUNTING

I steered our boat down the watery street in search of treasure.

Veggie zipped back and forth on the tiny deck. He held a pen cap to his eye like it was a telescope.

"All clear, Captain!" he called.

"Okay, Veggie," I said. "But stop rocking the boat so much."

Don't get me wrong. I was just as excited. No, maybe even more excited!

The storm had turned up all kinds of stuff that I normally don't see on the streets. Everywhere I looked, I spotted something new.

A slimy soap bar floated along. I also saw a long, leathery rope. It had a shiny metal attachment on one side and a bunch of holes punched into the other.

Then Veggie and I gawked as a mysterious piece of white fabric floated by. We had NO idea what that was.

As each object floated past us, I caught them all with my pie-rat treasure rod. I had made it by sticking another piece of A-B-C gum to the end of a string.

After all, there's absolutely nothing stickier than A-B-C gum!

We even met a critter—a yellow duck to be precise. It was wearing an eye patch, just like I was!

"Ahoy, fellow pie-rat!" we called out. But the duck didn't look our way. It just kept swimming past us.

Well, it was a shy pirate duck, but at least it looked the part.

The boat was starting to get crowded with all my discoveries. The night was still young, but this pie-rat was already rich with treasure!

"If only a whole pizza pie would float by too," Veggie said. Then he peered through the pen cap again.

"Oh no, Captain!" he shouted. "I spy a distressed ship ahead!"

I squinted toward where Veggie was pointing. But as we sailed closer, we realized the distressed ship was just a big piece of paper floating on the water's surface.

The paper was covered in colorful patterns and pictures. I wanted to take a closer look, but it was just beyond the reach of my sticky treasure rod.

I balanced on one leg and tried to lean as far as I could. The boat bobbed up and down dangerously.

"Let me help!" Veggie said. He grabbed onto my tail.

I leaned out a little farther, and it worked! I grabbed the paper and pulled it aboard.

"Whew! Thanks for your help, First Mate Veggie!" I said.

"My pleasure, Captain!" Veggie saluted me.

I wasn't sure if pie-rats saluted each other. But I smiled and saluted him back anyway.

Maybe it *was* nice to have my brother along on this treasure-hunting mission.

CHAPTER 6
A NEW KIND OF PIE

Veggie and I each took hold of one end of the wet paper. We carefully peeled apart the edges to unfold it.

Then we both gasped.

In big, bold letters, the paper read: PIE.

"I know what this is! It's a pizza pie treasure map!" Veggie squeaked.

Then my brother danced around and chanted, "Pizza pie! Pizza pie!"

"Hold on a second," I said. "How do you know that? I don't see any pizza anywhere on here."

We looked at the top, the bottom, the front, and the back of the paper.

The water had smudged the ink in some spots. But clearly there wasn't a single picture of pizza on it.

Instead, there were drawings of lots of round things with brown domed tops. We weren't sure exactly what they were, but our rat radar told us they looked like food.

Veggie and I stared at each other as a shocking thought entered both our minds at once.

Could there be a different kind of pie BESIDES pizza pie?

"Hey, check this out," I said, pointing at one of the pictures. The thing looked like it was covered with whipped cream on top, just like a cake.

"Veggie," I said, "you were right. We have stumbled upon a treasure map. A treasure map for some kind of SWEET PIE!"

We studied the map together. At the bottom of the page, there was a little drawing of some trees. A few blocks over, there was a road labeled "Seventh Street." On that road, someone had drawn a big red X.

And every pie-rat knows that X marks the spot!

Veggie held up his pen cap and pointed it every which way.

"Over there, Captain!" he said, pointing to the left. "I can see a park with lots of trees!"

I steered our boat, and we began to sail toward the park.

A short time later, we reached the park's entrance. It was strange to see all the trees with their roots covered up by water.

"Now, the map says that if we keep going a few blocks over, we'll get to Seventh Street and find the pies!" Veggie said.

My brother looked up at me with big eyes and asked, "Can we do it, Captain? Can we go look for this sweet treasure?"

Earlier, I had said that I wouldn't go out of my way for Veggie's pizza pie hunting. But now we were talking about an entirely different kind of pie.

Plus, Veggie had been pretty helpful so far as a first mate. I figured I owed him one.

"All right," I replied. "I, Captain Ratnip, declare our new destination: the PIE SHOP!"

CHAPTER 7
RIDING THE WAVES

Veggie and I set sail toward the pie shop. Our minds were swimming with thoughts about this mysterious sweet pie.

We wondered what it would taste like. Would it be like a pizza pie dough, but with candy toppings instead of savory toppings?

Or maybe the whole pie would be made of sweet candy, like a big, sticky gummy pie.

The more we imagined this sweet pie, the more we wanted it. RIGHT NOW!

But the boat was moving so slowly. We were weighed down by all my treasures, and the breeze had become nothing more than a gentle tickle.

We made our way through the waters at a snail's pace.

"Captain, I have an idea," Veggie said. He pointed to the side of the street. "Why don't we ride the waves over there?"

Rain gutters ran all along the sides of the street. They sucked in the water like big, thirsty creatures.

The water was moving faster over there, for sure. But Cookie had warned me to stay away from the gutters.

"Come on," Veggie pleaded. "It's going to be morning before we find our pies!"

"You're right," I said. "What's a pie-rat without a bit of choppy waters?"

I steered the boat toward the edge of the street. The current whooshed us along.

Our boat sped faster, and faster, and faster. It was a bumpy ride. But that made it even more fun!

"Woohoo!" Veggie and I cheered.

We were pie-rats sailing the high seas. We felt wild and free!

Then, suddenly, the boat hit an extra choppy wave.

"WHOA!" I shouted. I grabbed onto the wheel and tried to hold it steady.

Another wave sent our boat spinning. Veggie lost his balance and nearly fell over. The treasure map slipped out of his paws.

"No!" I screamed. "The map!"

I let go of the wheel. Veggie and I both lunged for the map.

But that turned out to be a very bad decision. Because without anyone to steer, the current carried us sideways and knocked us straight into a streetlight!

BOOM! The impact tossed the entire boat into the air.

"AAAHHHHHHH!" Veggie and I screamed, grabbing each other's paws.

Splash! We tumbled together into the water.

The current plunged us beneath the water's surface. My pie-rat eye patch flew off my face, and I didn't know which way was up or down.

I reached out a paw and grabbed hold of the first thing I touched. I hoped it was our boat, but it was just the leather rope I had collected.

Lucky for us, though, the rope had gotten tangled around the streetlight. Veggie and I managed to grab onto the rope and climb up the light pole.

Finally, we were safely out of the waves. But the rest of our ship was not so lucky.

There was nothing we could do as the current washed away the boat. Soon the treasure map and all my other treasures disappeared from sight.

CHAPTER 8
SHIPWRECKED

"Aw, RATS!" I yelled. "I just lost everything!"

Then I turned to Veggie.

"This is why you shouldn't have come on my adventure," I said. "Now we're stuck here, and it's all because you wanted to ride too close to the gutters!"

Veggie's whiskers drooped and his tail sagged. Water dripped from his wet fur.

"I just wanted to be part of your pie-rat crew," he said.

All the anger drained out of me. Now I felt bad. It was my turn for my whiskers to droop.

"Oh, Veggie, I'm sorry. I shouldn't have yelled at you," I said. "A pie-rat captain can't be a captain without his first mate."

I looked down from the streetlight and shivered. If only we could figure out a way to get back home.

But what was a shipwrecked pie-rat to do? All we had was the leather rope, which was still knotted around the streetlight.

I surveyed the area to see if there was anything nearby we could use as a ship. But what I found was something even more surprising.

Across the street was a shop with a polka-dotted awning. I pointed my noise in that direction and sniffed the air.

It smelled like wet trash. Yum! But I also detected the faintest hint of something sweet. Something even yummier!

I looked around and spotted the closest street sign. It said: SEVENTH STREET.

"Shiver me timbers!" I gasped. "Veggie, I think that's the pie shop!"

I couldn't believe it. The current had carried us all the way to our treasure!

"How are we going to cross all this water, though?" Veggie said. "The current is too fast. We're so close to the pies and yet so far away!"

But seeing the pie shop had filled me with new hope.

PIE-RAT FACT: When it comes to treasure, we rats never give up!

"Follow me," I said.

I slid down the pole until I was a tail's length above the water. I reached down  and untwisted the leather rope. Then I tied it tight around my waist.

I gave the metal end of the rope to Veggie.

"Veggie," I said, "you're my one and only first mate. Can I trust you to hold onto this rope and NEVER let go? No matter what?"

Veggie nodded with a serious face.

"I promise," he replied. "But what are you going to do, Captain Ratnip?"

"Just you watch," I said. Then I took a deep breath and dove straight into the water.

CHAPTER 9
THE SEVENTH STREET SWIM

I swam and I swam as hard as I could. Over the whooshing of the current, I could hear Veggie squeaking. But I couldn't stop to turn around or listen.

Like I said earlier, we rats are pretty good swimmers. But this was a wide stream, and the water was moving fast.

Every time I slowed down or started to drift off course, I felt a firm tug on the rope around my waist. It was Veggie, pulling me back on track and making sure I was safe.

Feeling his support gave me a burst of energy. I swam even harder.

I finally made it to the trash bags outside the pie shop. I leaped out of the water and climbed up.

"I did it!" I called to Veggie. "Now, are you ready?"

Veggie gave me a thumbs-up. Then he scurried down the streetlight and entered the water.

I pulled on the leather rope and reeled Veggie toward me. He held tight to the metal piece at the end of the rope.

"Heave ho!" I shouted. I gave the rope one more mighty tug.

Veggie joined me on the trash bag, safe and sound.

"Wow, that was amazing!" Veggie cheered.

"It's all thanks to this treasure," I said, patting the rope around my waist.

"Hey," Veggie said. "I don't know what the rope is used for, but it looks really good tied around your waist like that."

I looked down at the rope too. Who knew?

Now it was finally time to get our paws on the sweet pies we had been searching for.

And our noses told us they were right inside the trash can!

The sweet pies were big and round. Otherwise, they looked nothing like pizza pies. They were also tall and their bottoms sat inside metal tins.

My belly rumbled. I was starving after all that swimming.

We dove headfirst into the pies.

I bit into crunchy graham cracker crusts and gooey chocolate filling. I tasted tart lime and sweet cinnamon-y apple.

Every pie was different, and they were all *SWEET!*

Pretty soon my belly was bulging with pie. I had to loosen the leather rope around my waist to make more space!

"Wow, Captain Ratnip," Veggie said. "This treasure is even sweeter than my sweetest dreams!"

I wiped my whiskers and replied, "Aye aye, First Mate!"

CHAPTER 10
PIE, SWEET PIE

Veggie and I feasted like there was no tomorrow. But there were still so many pies left at the bottom of the trash can.

"If only we could bring them back home to share," I said. But we still didn't even have a way to get back home.

Veggie finished off another pie and tossed the empty tin aside. And then a light bulb went off in my head.

"Veggie!" I said. "What if we use this tin as our new boat?"

We lifted it up, carefully rolled it to the edge of the trash can, and pushed it into the water.

And guess what? The tin didn't sink!

"If it floats, it's a boat!" I declared. "Hooray!"

We loaded as much leftover pie as we could fit onto our new boat. Then we climbed aboard and let the tide carry us down Seventh Street.

The journey home was smooth sailing. This time we were careful to avoid the gutters, of course.

"How long do you think The City will be underwater like this?" Veggie asked.

"I don't know," I said. "Maybe it'll all be gone when we wake up tomorrow night."

"Well," Veggie said. He scooched closer to me. "Thanks for letting me come with you. I'm glad I got to go on this adventure."

I smiled and wrapped an arm around Veggie to give him a hug.

"I am too," I said. "You're the best first mate any pie-rat could ask for."

When we got home, Cookie and all our siblings oohed and ahhed over the sweet pies.

They were a little soggy from the boat ride, but they still tasted amazing. Anchovy ate so fast that all her whiskers got covered in whipped cream!

After our feast, I dragged the pie tin boat up to my treasure room.

I had lost nearly all the knicks and knacks from tonight. But it was okay, because I had gotten even MORE precious treasures instead.

Sweet pies. A happy tummy. And a very special adventure with my little brother!

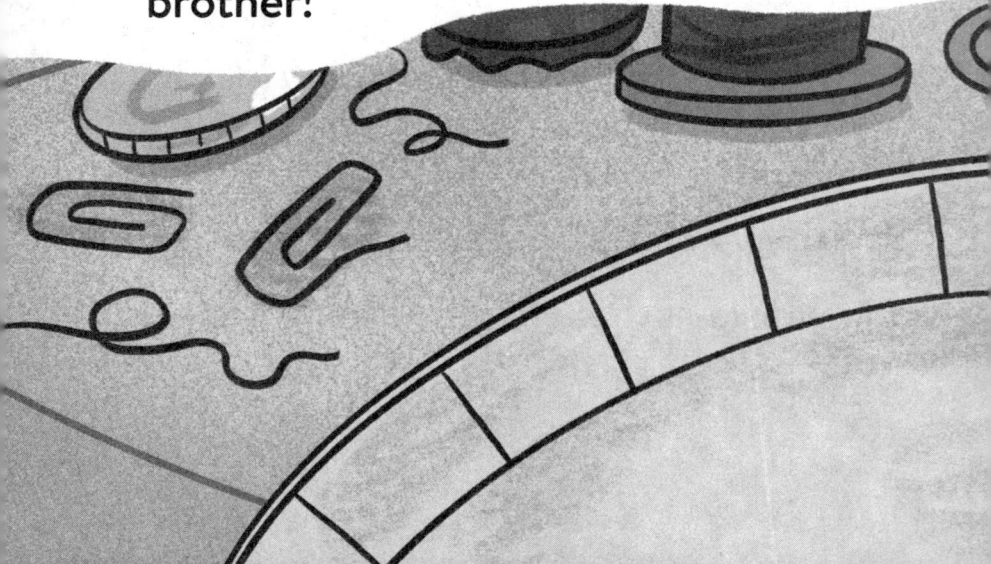

Here's a peek at Ratnip's next adventure!

POP QUIZ: What is something you can see anytime, anywhere in The City?

If you answered "trash," you're correct.

But there's also another correct answer.

And that is: CONSTRUCTION!

Everywhere you go, there is construction, construction, and more construction. The City is constantly growing and changing.

Sometimes humans fix up a place or build a brand-new building. Or they'll even tear them down.

Rat Fact: Construction is very important business for us rats, too.

Whenever a new construction site pops up, my older siblings, Pepperoni and Marg, scurry off to go visit it. They always told me I was too young to tag along.

But tonight? Tonight was a magical night. I was finally joining my older siblings and becoming a member of the Night Crew!

If you don't know what the Night Crew does, don't feel bad. Neither do I! But I'm sure it's super cool and important . . . and only for big rats like me.

Pepperoni, Marg, and I ate an early breakfast. The sun was just setting outside.